Chasing The Dragon

Chasing The Dragon by

Jesse Clemente

Published by Jesse Clemente Books

JesseClementeBooks@gmail.com

© 2017 Jesse Clemente

Cover by Christoper Soprano

Headshot: © 2017 Lance Sakowski

Dedicated to Laura, Ella, and Kali

Table of Contents

1
The Beginning

The crispness in the air made it one of those mornings that you long for in the midst of the sweltering summer's heat. The sun had begun to glisten off the ocean and unto the face of a defeated man who lay still in his goose bumped arms as he was trying to muster enough drive just to open his guitar case. Jack finally committed himself to opening up the orange felted case and he pulled out his acoustic adorned with hummingbirds, as they lay forever etched into the pick guard. Jack not only liked it for it's tone, but also it's cherry sunburst finish that resembled the exact tint of whiskey. He sat on that bench and unleashed his despair through his guitar until the sun began to emerge and beat against his back.

Jack's whole world has recently been turned upside down. It was coming up on two years that he was shot in the line of duty while making a drug buy in Bedford Stuyvesant Brooklyn while working undercover in narcotics. His shoulder was torn up by the gunshot but by God's grace, it only took one surgery and 6 months of physical therapy to get most of his mobility back. He was then forced to retire with a disability pension and pick up the pieces of his new life that would continue to spiral downward. His brother Christopher had overdosed from a Heroin and Fentanyl combination while living in Williamsburg Brooklyn right after the shooting. Christopher experimented with drugs since high school but Jack had no idea that he was battling a Heroin addiction. As far as Jack knew, Christopher was living the bachelor's dream. He had a good advertising job in Manhattan and lived in a luxury apartment in Williamsburg Brooklyn. Jack spent the past decade risking his life on the front lines in the war against drugs and he couldn't fathom how his own brother got hooked on that junk.

During his recovery at home after the shooting and Christopher's death, he began to notice that Lauren was building an addiction to alprazolam. Lauren, his now estranged wife, was prescribed them to treat her anxiety after Jack's shooting. As most of these stories end, she got hooked on them and went into treatment for a month. The addiction and her bouts of relapse after her affair with opiates destroyed their relationship and she found a new boyfriend. Needless to say, her new boyfriend Johnny was another ex-junkie/dealer that was arrested at least a dozen times. Against Jack's better judgment, he and Lauren made the decision that she would take their daughter Isabel down to Florida to live with her parents after she was consistently sober for a little over six months. Jack felt that Lauren was now stable enough with her sobriety that she could care for Isabel. He also knew that Lauren needed Isabel as inspiration to stay sober. Jack was sure that her parents would intervene if they found her relapsing. Lauren, Isabel, and her new boyfriend, Johnny, moved down to Jupiter Florida. Jack hated the idea of being so far away from Isabel but he needed to hang back in Brooklyn to fulfill his secret agenda. Jack was poised to find those responsible for Christopher's death.

He packed up his guitar and took in the smell of the sea through his nostrils as he closed his eyes and asked for God to help him through this tumultuous time. He then walked over to his 95 *Chevy* pickup with guitar case in hand and gently placed the guitar in the bed. Jack closed the rear hatch then continued into the driver seat, started the ignition, and began to drive a few blocks down to his parent's Rockaway Beach home. The fabric of the torn bench seat wicked away the beading sweat off his back. Upon walking through the front door of his folks' house, the aroma of sirloin steak and garlic frying up in a saucepan automatically triggered nostalgia. Jack's dad, Manny, was sitting at the head of the table with his shirt off and elbows on the table as his mother, Maria, stood by the stove marinating the skirt steak in both garlic and love.

"How was your day today?" Manny asked.

"It was alright…I went by the beach and mellowed out."

"How have you been feeling?"

"Everything is fine."

"Your mom tells me you are moving in to Christopher's apartment," Manny said condescendingly as Maria began to violently sob as she salted the steak.

"It's the right move, I wanna take it in before I put it past me."

"You're upsetting your mom. Change the subject!" Manny exclaimed as he walked over to Maria and massaged her shoulders.

Jack simultaneously questioned if he was making the right decision. His brother was dead and his ex-junk box ex-wife took his daughter down to Florida to live with an ex-convict. Also, the career he loved was now a monthly check and a pocket full of surreal memories that left him yearning for the next dose of adrenaline, his drug of choice. Jack knew he would get his next dose shortly for he was hell bent on revenge and finding who sold Christopher that hot dose of dope.

"Steak sandwiches are ready!" Maria exclaimed as she moved over to Jack to give him a kiss on his forehead. Jack spent another hour or so eating sandwiches and talking politics with his parents. After the meal, Maria began washing the dishes as Manuel plopped himself on the couch. Jack thanked his folks for the meal as he gave his mom a kiss on her cheek.

"How come you don't stay here with us?" Maria asked.

"I like staying in Christopher's apartment, it makes me feel a little closer to him." Jack responded.

"Well, you call me when you get there," Maria demand as she fought back tears.

"Will do. I'm gonna take the bike for a few days, the truck is leaking transmission fluid again."

"You be careful on that motorcycle Jack," Maria lectured.

"Always," he said after kissing her on the cheek.

Maria blessed herself with the sign of the cross as a tears slowly dripped down her face. Jack gave his father a hug and continued down into the garage. As Jack walked into the garage, the red and rust patina glowed and drew him in closer. He reminisced of the day he and Christopher picked up the bike from a widow's barn in upstate New York. It was Christopher's

1946 *Chief* in all its glory. Jack always though of this machine as the embodiment of freedom and an old-fashioned piece of Americana. Jack opened up the garage and pulled the *Chief* out of garage. He laid down the kickstand and pulled out the kicker pedal, as he simultaneously doubted whether or not the bike would start. Jack raised the pedal and fired down with one quick and forceful thrust forward. She then began to purr.

As Jack returned to the garage to retrieve Christopher's old half-helmet, he noticed a fine and golden surprise. There laid a strand of Christopher's hair. Jack picked the hair and clenched it in his clammy fist as he returned to the *Chief*. Jack held in the clutch and put the motorcycle into gear as he rolled the throttle with his thumb and pointer finger as not to release the memento Christopher had left behind. As Jack turned onto the highway, he opened up the throttle and the cascade of the setting sun ricocheted off the ocean's surface delivering him the feeling of serendipity. He then opened up his still clenched fist and watched as the strand of his late-brothers hair flew off into the wind. It was one of those rare and surreal moments that remind us of the beauty of being alive.

Jack roared down the Belt Parkway as he took in the freedom he could only achieve by being on two wheels. The blare of a police siren and blinding strobe lights trailed swiftly behind him. Jack then pulled over and waited for the Officer to greet him with the spiel. He heard the car door close and the subsequent footsteps. Once the Officer walked up, Jack heard the officer call him by name and Jack recognized him to be Matt, his old pal from high school.

"How the hell are you?" Matt asked as he removed his mirrored Ray Bans from his face.
"I'm fine, just adjusting to retirement and trying to figure out the next chapter."
"I heard you got hurt real bad. You're lucky to be alive."
"They haven't found a way to kill me yet." Jack chuckled as a feeling of ambivalence overcame him partly because he was amazed that he survived being shot and yet partly because he wished he didn't.
"I'm real sorry about Christopher, by the way," Matt unsteadily stated.
"Yeah, Me too," Jack responded.

Jack and Matt said their goodbyes and as Matt walked back to his patrol car, Jack gave the kick-start on the *Chief* one swift kick and it fired up in with the intonation of a beast roaring from the depths of hell. The only problem was that for Jack…. Hell was closer to him than for most folks.

Without a parking spot in sight, Jack elected to park on the sidewalk in front of Christopher's apartment building. It was eerie walking through the door of his late brother's apartment. Although the apartment was neat, it showed signs that it was still lived in. There were still a few dishes in the sink and the television in the living room was still on. Jack dropped his duffle bag on the living room floor and crashed on the couch. He noticed that his foot had knocked off a small object from the coffee table when he threw his foot up on it.

Upon further investigation, it appeared to be matchbook emblazoned with logo for *Roxy's Gentleman's Club.* He lit a cigarette with a match from the book and took a puff while studying the matchbook.

He woke up the following morning and immediately started towards the bathroom. Showering and getting the fuck out of that mausoleum of an apartment felt like a good idea. A feeling of eeriness smothered the place, as if Christopher would walk through the front door at any moment. Jack peeled off his shirt and stared at his reflection through the mirrored medicine cabinet. The first thing he noticed was the entry wound from the bullet that went through his chest. A culmination of anger and self-pity began to emerge through his pores and heat the surface of his skin. That bullet wound was more than just a scar. It was a constant reminder of the moment that his life began to spiral downward. A fit of rage consumed him as he punched the glass with rapid haymakers causing shards of glass to rain upon the bathroom. The blunt force rattled the medicine cabinet ajar and allowed Jack to see what lurked on the shelf behind the glass. There was a glassine envelope that was stamped with the image of a red dragon that contained heroin. He examined it as blood and shards of glass flowed into the sink's drain.

2

Making New Friends

The smell of pastries and coffee wafting in the air lured Jack into a quaint little coffee shop on Grand Street. He sat down in the seating outside the shop as he nursed his Americano. Two guys in their early 30s that appeared to be strikingly identical walk down the street deeply engrossed in conversation until they intermittently smiled and laughed before resuming the rest of the conversation. Jack imagined that they were brothers. A feeling of deprivation consumed Jack as he studied these gentlemen as they walked passed the cafe. His best friend, his brother, became some addict that was found lifeless on the floor of an hourly rate hotel room, he said to himself in loathing self-pity. His mind began to wander as he conceded how Christopher's untimely death demanded more than the open and shut investigation that the cops conducted. The cops didn't give a fuck about some junkie that the cleaning lady found covered in bile with a needle still stuck in arm. He needed answers and someone to blame...someone to hate. Someone to unleash vengeance upon. He contemplated getting up after finishing his last swig of coffee until a vagrant approached him. This fellow pushed a shopping cart overflowing in scrap metal. The cart began to pass by Jack until it came to a halt.

"Excuse me sir, but do you happen to have some change?"

"I don't have any change but I got an empty seat, come take a load off."

"That sounds pretty good right about now, I've been on the move since eight o'clock this morning." Jack then pointed to the seat across from him.

"Thank you for the gesture. You are a kind fellow."

"Don't mention it, you hungry?"

"I sure am." Jack then gestured to the waitress and she approached with judgmental eyes.

"Can I get you something?" asked the waitress. Jack then nodded up and down in an approving manner.

"I'll take a ham and cheese sandwich."

"Coming right up," she said as she simultaneously scribbled down his order.

"I'm Abe, pleasure to meet you."

"The pleasure is all mine. How is the day going so far?"

"You know, a typical day in New York…Herds of fancy motherfuckers looking down at their phones while the world passes them by. I remember the days when you would walk down a block and pickup three new friends. Not no more. Anyways, most people avoid me thinking I'm some crack head or some shit. I don't do that no more. I been clean ever since a few years back."

"God bless, sobriety ain't easy."

"Tell me about it."

"Lemme ask you a question seeing that you got your ear to the street and all."

"That I do, hit me.

"Ham and cheese sandwich?" the food runner asked while presenting a plate bearing a ham and cheese sandwich on ciabatta bread.

"You heard of some dope called the red dragon?"

"A few fellas at the shelter overdosed a while back and I heard some jazz that the dope they was taking was pretty strong. It was called red dragon. That's all I know. I don't know who fucks with it or nothin. Only heard of it that one time," Abe said as he devoured the sandwich in no more than four bites.

"Thanks for the info Abe. It was great meeting you."

"Pleasure is all mine," Abe said as he wiped his mouth with the paper napkin as he stood up from the table. "I gotta get back to finding some more scrap. Been competitive lately with the economy and all."

"I wish you the best, take care."

"You too, thanks for the lunch."

"Anytime."

Later that evening, Jack figured he didn't have much to go on so he would go to the *Roxy Gentleman Club* and see if he could ruffle some feathers there. He rationalized that if all else failed, it had been a while since he saw a good set of tits. Once inside the club, Jack sat upon a stool and perched up next to the bar. He ordered bourbon and asked the bartender to change some bills for singles. The house music and fluorescent lights added to an extra level of sleaziness to the joint as fake asses and breasts jiggled to the beat blaring from the speakers.

The most attractive dancer on the stage was a brunette with olive tone skin. She was about 5'8" but the transparent stilettos probably brought her to a whopping 6'2". She was wearing a white guarder belt and had a set of nipples that faced towards the heavens, as her bra lay flipped down towards earth as soon as her set started. Some jerk with a nylon tracksuit and salt and pepper hair began to saturate her with singles. Something then happened that caught Jack's eye. This gentleman clenched his fist and placed a small object in her bra where her plump left breast defied the laws of gravity. Jack sat and observed for a while. The next thing he knew, those nipples where protruding through white lace and into Jack's face. She introduced herself as Candy and asked Jack his name. He gave her a fictitious name, as he was accustomed to doing while working undercover.

"You want to come upstairs for a dance in the VIP room?" Candy asked.
"Sounds like a party to me," Jack responded. Candy then walked off the stage and around the bar to Jack. She then grabbed him by the hand

and escorted him down the corridor into the hazy stench of cigar smoke and pussy.

The private room was nothing more than brown leather couch guarded by a black curtain. Candy straddled Jack and began to shake her ass in a circular motion over his oil-slicked jeans. He then reached into her bra and felt the waxiness of a glassine envelope. She was under the impression that he was just catching a feel as he snatched the bag of dope from inside her bra. Upon recovering the glassine, Jack grabbed Candy by the waist and took her off his lap.

"What's the matter? You don't want the VIP package?" Candy disappointingly asked.
"Nah, your boney ass has been digging in my legs."
"Fuck you asshole!" Candy exclaimed.

"You wish," Jack said sarcastically. He then got up and walked down the stairs passing business men in suits as they negotiated prices for sexual favors with the skimpily clad show girls. Jack then entered the bathroom and saw the cool guy with the tracksuit that gave Candy the bag of dope. Jack approached the sink and removed the glassine of heroin from his pocket. He then started to flick the bag to loosen up the tan granular powder as his target simultaneously turned away from the urinal.

"What the fuck are you doing?"

"What does it look like I'm doing?" Jack shrugged.

"You are gonna get us all locked up."

"My bad brother, I'm trying to loosen up my last bump and my connect isn't answering the fucking phone."

"Put that shit away. What do you need?"

"Two bombs," street terminology for twenty bags of heroin.

Jack then handed him one hundred and eighty dollars as he in turn handed Jack twenty glassines containing tan powdery devastation.

"How much money is here?"

"One-Eighty."

"It's two hundred, my man."

"That's all I got."

"Aight, just get me next time. Take down my math; I'm up all-day and everyday. I'm Tito by the way."

"I'm Jack, I'm gonna text you now so you have my number. If this shit is good, I'll hit you up again," he said as to not sound too desperate. He always made it a point to create the illusion with the dealers that they needed him more than he needed them. The drug addict and drug dealer relationship is a volatile one like every other relationship in life, a constant power struggle to be the alpha. Being perceived as a push over can cost you your life in the streets, because the only people that are desperate are cops, informants, and fiends. None of them get respect in the drug game. Jack wanted to portray himself as a low level dealer that used. His intention was to buy up a little bit to see if Tito would turn him on to some other connects. Connects that may have been possibly responsible for Christopher's untimely death.

Jack stored Tito's number in his phone and walked outside. He then started up the *Chief* with one swift kick. A woman's voice could be heard yelling incoherently after he dropped the bike into gear and began to pull away.

"Give me back my fucking dope you jerk off," Candy screamed as she ran through the parking lot wearing nothing but her panties and stilettos. Jack looked behind him while pulling away to see what the commotion was all about when Candy's stiletto hit the sidewalk the wrong way and she crashed, face first into the sidewalk.

The next morning Jack lit up a smoke and played some vinyl on Christopher's vintage record player. Jack checked his prepaid cell phone and saw a text from Tito. He threw on some flip-flops and decided to go for a walk. He stopped and grabbed a coffee at the French bakery up the block. He poured in the milk and couldn't help as to gaze into the cup as the cream spread outward and began to overtake the abyss of black coffee. He then crossed the street and parked his ass on a bench as he watched people walk by. Jack loved people watching. As a teenager, he would just pick a bench and scrupulously observe people coming and going. It was more than that though. He loved to study them. You can really learn a lot by studying people's behavior…how they walk, how they talk, and most importantly….How they interact with each other. An understanding of people, a love for acting, and the ability to be a master manipulator made Jack an undercover that excelled in every task presented in front of him. Most people would think that one would be at a certain level of serenity when immersed in the corona of the summer's day sun overlooking the East river. Not Jack, for he was brooding and planning.

Jack knew that he wasn't going to find *El Chapo* but the whole point of this plan that was beginning to manifest was to find the low level piece of shit that poisoned his brother and get payback. The only problem was that Jack no longer had anything to lose and he still didn't know how this justice would be served. The plan was to call Tito the following day and order up a sleeve, one-hundred glassines, of dope. It was a little bold to order up that much so soon but Jack wanted to know what kind of player Tito was. Jack's immediate course of action was the only thing he really had to plan out. Buying drugs was the easy part for he had spent his entire career cultivating that skill. The rest of the morning was spent gazing at the hole in which the World Trade Center once stood and self-reflecting at the hole within his soul.

Jack awoke the following day around noon. He turned on a pot of pumpkin roast coffee and before the pot was filled, he had mustered up enough gall to dial Tito's number.

"Who's this?"

"Jack…I need some work."

"What do you need?"

"A sleeve for seven-hundred."

"Eight-hundred is the best I can do."

"Are you kidding me?"

"You want it or not?"

"Yeah."

"Meet me at the Diner on Metropolitan in an hour."

"I'll see you in an hour."

Jack then hung up the phone and poured a cup of the piping hot coffee. The first sip burnt his mouth and he realized he didn't have time to let it cool. He then went downstairs and into the garage to fire up the *Chief*.

Jack rumbled up on the sidewalk in front of the diner and kicked down the stand. He couldn't help but notice some elderly fellow nervously peering through the window in an attempt to uncover what had caused all that uncanny ruckus. Jack walked over to the far booth so no one could get the drop on him. A waitress wearing a teal uniform that resembled the color of hospital walls greeted him and handed him a menu. Jack told her that he already knew what he wanted...two eggs sunny side up with ham steak and an OJ. She wrote down his order and walked through the kitchen's double doors. The sound of squeaky brakes synchronized with the kitchen doors as they swooshed closed. The sound compelled jack to peruse through the blinds adjacent to the booth and he saw a late 80s model *Deville* pull up next to the *Chief*.

Tito began to creep up the front entrance as he furtively scanned his head back and forth. Jack patted his side to affirm that he was carrying his snub nose .38. It was the one with a scratched out serial number in case shit went bad and he had to put a hole in Tito's head. The kitchen bell rang as Tito aimlessly walked past the corridor lined with booths. Jack nodded and Tito helped himself to a seat.

"Would you like to see a menu, hun?" the waitress asked as she placed Jack's platter of eggs and bacon on the table.
"No disrespect but the streets are the streets. You a cop?"

"Don't insult me. I work for a living," Jack said.

"I just had to ask. It's entrapment if they don't tell you that they are a cop."

"I heard some shit like that too," Jack deceptively affirmed as he internalized his laughter.

"The shit I got is fire. A few people overdosed off it. So just be careful." Jack smiled as he gripped the handle of his serrated edge knife that was covered with yolk. He masked his hatred for Tito and his disregard for life as he gloated about those that succumbed to his fatal batch of dope.

"Lets get on with it, my eggs are getting cold," Jack said. Tito then handed Jack a black shopping bag underneath the table. Jack slightly opened the bag to make sure it was all there and then he placed the cash underneath the plate of toast.

"Boof it, the boys are outside," Tito said, implicating that he wanted Jack to place the bag between his ass cheeks because the cops were out front.

"My man, no disrespect, but I know how to handle my business. If this shit is good, I'll be in touch." Tito got up without responding and left the diner while scanning left and right.

Jack paid the bill and left a few minutes after Tito. He saw some beat cops hanging on the corner but Jack gave zero fucks because he knew damn well that unless they worked narcotics, most cops didn't know what a drug deal looked like and the cops that did were afraid to be the next victims of political agendas and the next face on the news that would spark civil unrest. The streets knew that too and the drug game was reaping the rewards. He reminisced and asked himself how many drug deals he did as an undercover while right in front of uniformed police. The overwhelmingly sad truth was that they often had no clue what was going down. Jack walked over to the *Chief* and unbuckled the saddlebag, placed the plastic bag inside that contained the dope, and buckled it back up. He then mounted the *Chief* and gave the kick-start one swift kick. She fired right up and he took off like a bat out of hell. He knew no one could stop him now.

He rode back to his folks' house in the Rockaways and immediately darted toward the backyard. He began examining the heroin and couldn't help but notice that these bundles of dope had all different stamps on them. It appeared that Tito was a low level guy that needed to get it from a few different dealers to fill the order. Jack knew that he could use him though. The assorted dope was also an indicator that Tito's name was good in the neighborhood and that people would drop their guard if he used him as a reference.

Jack retrieved a can of lighter fluid from the shed and began to squirt it into the pit. He lit a match and the flames simultaneously arose from the culmination of firewood and accelerant. He sifted through his recently acquired bundles of heroin and took a second look. It was in hope of finding the red dragon but it was to no avail. Jack put the bundles back in the shopping bag and the flames of the fiery pit were now strong enough to sustain themselves. He chucked the bag into the fire and continued into the side entrance of the house. After returning to the yard with a six-pack, he pulled up a folding chair next to the fire pit and sipped the frothy suds as the flames reflected off his pupils. He began to ponder what his plan was considering the fact that he was purchasing narcotics for a hefty sum then destroying it. The more he fretted over it, the more the realization came through that he did not know what his intentions were. He knew that he was close to finding out who was responsible for giving his brother a hot batch but he was unsure of what he was to do once he found out some answers. Now that he wasn't a cop any longer, there were no more rules, regulations, or laws to follow. Death was the retribution to be dealt and he knew how to get away with murder. He was privy to hundreds of homicide investigations and understood the nuances of how these investigations are conducted and how perpetrators are caught. Jack knew he was smart enough to get away with it but he had never killed and he was frightened of who he might become. The mortal sin of killing would forever change how he perceived himself. Thoughts of life, death, and payback ran through his mind the rest of the evening as he crushed beers and stared into the radiance of the flames, dancing in the abyss of the pit.

3

Making Moves

The stale summer air seeped through the bedroom windows of the railroad apartment in the old three-story walk up off the corner of South 3rd Street and Havemeyer. Sounds of vintage mopeds and construction crews building sterile buildings to house New York's upper echelon radiated through the archaic panes of glass, caked with layers of paint coats that were applied several times over throughout the decades. These decades brought more tote bags and skinny jeans and less gun toting and chalk outlines in Williamsburg Brooklyn although drugs and violence still had their place in the gentrified neighborhood.

The sound of cranes awoke Tito Rodriguez from his slumber. He rose from his bed and walked into the kitchen. Seated were his three little girls eating pancakes and drinking orange juice. Interestingly enough, they were seated around the table in age order….Three, Five, and Six years of age. Tito walked up to each one of them and gave them a kiss on their forehead.

"Good morning, Papi," the girls chanted in unison.

"Good morning my little angels." Tito was glad that his children didn't have to eat a tomato and half an egg for breakfast like he did when he was growing up. Life wasn't easy on the street when Tito was growing up and he refused to have to let his children go through the same obstacles. The only thing he knew was the streets and that was the only means he had to provide for his family. Although, he was doing what he had to do, the thing that kept him awake most nights was that if you live by the sword, you die by the sword.

Tito got dressed and walked to the bodega to get a coffee. All the neighborhood kids were hanging out front of the bogie as Tito walked through the door and sounded off the door chimes. Pablo greeted Tito and promptly started pouring Tito his morning cup of coffee. The salsa music playing from the radio and the first cup of cafe got Tito ready to start his day. He walked down the street to South Second Street and saw a few of the fellas sitting around their makeshift domino table off the sidewalk curb. He sat down in an empty folding chair adjacent to the table. Seated across from him was Angelo. He was about six foot two and had the words "Fuck the world" tattooed on the right side of his neck. His braided hair ended right before the scar that was embedded upon his bare chest. It was clearly an old knife wound.

"You sold all them shirts?" Angelo asked.

"Yeah, I need to order more."

"That was quick."

"People saying that batch is fire," Tito said as he handed Angelo an envelope underneath the table.

"It's the best, every fiend is looking for *EL FUEGO*. Product recognition my man. You see, I put straight fentanyl in every couple of bundles. This way the word gets out that a few cats OD and they figure they getting bang for their buck," Angelo explained.

"I see."

"You caught me before my re-up, that's why I didn't have the full order yesterday. I'll be whole by tonight." Angelo continued.

"It's all good. I can wait till later for the big thing but I need a few bundles to hold these fiends over for now," Tito responded.

Angelo abruptly retrieved his phone from his pocket and walked a few paces away from the domino table. It was far enough that Tito couldn't make out what he was saying. Angelo then hung up the phone and continued a few feet up the block. Shortly thereafter, a female Hispanic with bleached blonde hair and a fire engine red halter-top emerged on the sidewalk. She was pushing a baby stroller with a baby boy no older than 6 months of age. She approached Angelo and gave him a kiss on the cheek. Angelo then waved over to Tito indicating that he wanted him to come over. Tito approached the seemingly young family and the female picked up the baby. She handed the baby boy to Tito and he lulled him in an effort to console him. The innocent baby boy's mom then kissed Tito on the cheek and whispered in his ear. "It's in his diaper." Tito then retrieved a plastic sandwich bag wrapped containing a couple of bundles (stacks of heroin glassines wrapped in sets of ten, typically with a rubber band) from the diaper and placed it in his pants pocket. Tito then placed the child into the stroller. Angelo and the woman then left the location and pushed the baby carriage up the block. The bleach blonde woman then gave the child to an elderly woman that appeared to be the child's grandmother. A black *Chevy* with tinted windows rolled past the block as the screeching worn brakes could be heard amongst the lively block of shirtless children riding their bicycles and old men playing dominos with their Sunday's best in the midst of the sweltering heat. A child no older than 12 years old rode his bicycle mid block and whistled and yelled, "The boys are out," signifying the cops were in the area. Everyone then began to casually evacuate the pestilence of South 3rd Street.

Jack was sitting in Christopher's old apartment perusing through his old record collection and magazines that lay organized in the corner of his living room when the phone started ringing. Jack picked up the phone and saw that it was a blocked number.

"Hello?"

"It's me Tito. I got new work."

"How much for a sleeve?" That was street terminology for one-hundred glassine of heroin.

"Six-hundred."

"Cool."

"Meet me in front of the bogie and Humboldt and Moore at 8 pm."

"See you then."

Jack knew that Tito wasn't stupid enough to link up with him carrying that much dope next to the projects. Tito would be asking to get locked up and Jack took it as a good sign. Jack predicted that Tito was going to bring him to an inside location considering how much product was going to change hands. Moreover, Jack knew that Tito's connect would be present and want to meet him considering how much Jack was buying.

Jack roared down Graham Avenue and Broadway about a block away from the meeting point because he figured he wouldn't have eyes on the *Chief* and that bike was as good as gone if he left it unattended. Graham Avenue was a well-illuminated strip of businesses that was frequently patrolled by the police and he knew that it would be good there. The cuchi frito shop was open late and he figured the amount of pedestrian traffic coming to and from the restaurant would deter any potential thief. He dismounted the bike and walked up the block in front of the bodega at the corner of Humboldt and Moore. Jack then heard a whistle come from inside of the bodega. Tito was wearing bathing suit shorts, chocletas, and a tank top that showed off his flabby arms. One of which had "Muneca" scrawled across it in faded jailhouse ink. Muneca means baby doll in Spanish and Jack couldn't help but wonder if Tito was someone's baby doll when he was locked up or it was one of his old lady's nicknames. Tito told

Jack to follow behind him. Jack fell behind Tito as they marched over to the complex. Tito kept looking furtively for police by bobbing his head left and right repeatedly. Jack thought to himself, "Doesn't this guy realize he looks suspect looking all around like that?" They then walked over to a building that had scaffolding adorned to the facade that impeded the sign indicating the building number. Jack always made it a point to know his location when he was working undercover in case he needed help, especially when entering the projects. Tito held open the door and they then walked into the lobby. Jack was trying to look at mailboxes or city permits to discern his location while they were waiting for the elevator. "Ring". The elevator landed and the doors slung open before he could figure out the address. The elevator was empty if you excluded the pool of urine and cigar guts in the center of the elevator floor. Tito and Jack continued to the corner apartment once off at the sixth floor. The door read apartment "6A" and was dented with circular imprints near the locking mechanism. "Looks like narcotics rammed this door down before," Jack concluded. Tito then knocked on the door with a rhythmic variation to alert whomever was inside. Angelo cracked open the door with just enough space that allowed him to size up Jack from the bottom of his boots up to the tip of the handkerchief on his head. "Come in," Angelo said in an apprehensive yet authoritative voice. Once inside, Angelo turned four deadbolt locks in the locking position. Jack made a mental notation of every lock that slid into position. This practice was reinforced through his days as an undercover. Those deadbolts could delineate with what ease your backup team could safely extract you from the apartment if the situation went sideways while making a drug buy. This time there was no backup team but Jack reminded himself that it was always just he and God when doing undercover work. Moreover, it was just he and God, doing God's work.

Once through the fortress door, Angelo gave Tito a hug and stared Jack up and down.

"Who is this?" Angelo asked.

"He's good people."

"I don't know him," Angelo said while endearingly placing his arm around Jack in an effort to feel for a wire.

"If you're Tito's friend, you're my friend," Angelo chuckled.

Jack and Tito sat down into a droopy gray cloth sofa. Jack observed a male in his late 20s sitting on the living room floor opposite them, as his back lay pressed up against the filthy wall. A rubber hose was choked up around his bicep as he used his free hand to push the plunger of a hypodermic needle burrowed into the crevice of his arm. The cooked brown dope tangoed with blood inside the chamber of the needle as his big blue eyes locked with Jack's. His head then nodded as those pearly blues dissipated into an abyss. Jack suddenly had "oh shit" moment. He knew this poor sap passed out on the floor of the trap house. He was a friend of Christopher's. Christopher, Adam, and Jack had gone to a concert together a few years back at the *Williamsburg Waterfront*. Adam also knew that Jack was a cop. Not only would this vigilante case be over if Adam ratted, but Jack knew his life could be over as well.

Angelo took a seat in a sofa that was situated parallel to them. He then retrieved half the order, five bundles already banded together and stamped with assorted images, and handed them to Jack. A coffee table was nestled up against Angelo's legs. On this table laid a mixing bowl containing some loose heroin and a few dozen empty glassine envelopes. Angelo would dip a small scalpel-like instrument into the bowl and pour it into the glassine envelope. From there, he would flick the glassine as to get the powder to the bottom of the glassine. The next phase of the process was to make a trifold bend into the loaded glassine and place a piece of tape unto the two flaps to seal the envelope. Adjacent to a scale and a bag of potato chips on the far end of the table laid a red ink pad with a stamp resting above it. Angelo then pushed the stamp into the pad and began blotting the image of nautical stars across the faces of the glassine envelopes. The red ink stained Angelo's hands as he pressed firmly across the envelopes. The first twenty stamps felt like an eternity and Jack was eager to get the fuck out of dodge.

"You don't have to worry about all that, I'll take em like that," Jack calmly said.

"You sure?"

"Yeah, I'm good."

"Just be careful with this dope, it's real strong," Angelo lectured.

"Could you do me one favor before you leave?"

"Sure."

"Take this fucking dope head with you. Just leave him in the stairwell."

"We got him, Angie," Tito overzealously exclaimed in an attempt to kiss Angelo's ass.

"It's hard to find good help. My customers were calling me all day telling me they never got their packages. This asshole was getting high on my shit all day," Angelo yelled while throwing his hands in the air.

Angelo then dumped the loose glassine envelopes and a handful of loose rubber bands in a shopping bag as to make sure Jack had all the required stationary supplies. Jack then handed Angelo the cash. "We are all good", Angelo said as he shuffled through the last hundred-dollar bill. Angelo then walked over to Adam as he lay passed out on the trap house floor. There was a loud thud as Angelo kicked him in the rib cage in an effort to wake him up. He didn't budge. Angelo then walked over to the front door and unlocked each off the four-deadbolt locks. Jack and Tito then got up off the couch in tandem and walked over to Adam to pry him off the floor. They each took an arm and walked him toward the front door as Tito twisted the knob and opened the door. Once inside the stairwell, they placed him across the cold gray concrete staircase of stairwell B. Tito then jogged back into apartment 6A and closed the door. The sequence of the deadbolts engaging could be heard through the closed stairwell door.

Jack immediately felt for Adam's pulse and could not find one. He knew he was without oxygen long enough that the chances of him coming back were slim to none. Then it occurred to him…. This could be his wild card. Jack went into the shopping bag that was crammed inside of his pocket and removed one of the glassine envelopes that was stamped with the red nautical star. He then unsealed the glassine and placed it into Adam's pocket. He took a glance into Adam's open lifeless eyes and imagined how Christopher looked during his final moments at which he walked into the next world. He snapped out of it when an idea crossed his mind.

Jack scoped out the address of the building as he exited the building. He then calmly walked across the street and took a load off in the bus shelter. He then observed Tito exit the building a few minutes later. Tito still had the same culpable look as if he was up to no good as he peered back and forth. Jack had spared Tito because he knew that he was an asset that would plug him into the neighborhood and allow him to cultivate more connects with the bigger fish. Jack knew that he was in the right place and dealing with the right people. He wasn't certain that he was going to run into the same dope that killed Christopher but he knew that he was following the right leads. Jack walked back across the street and approached a payphone as Tito walked off the block.

"911 What is your emergency?"
"My grandson is choking."
"Where is your grandson?"
"372 Bushwick Avenue Apartment 6A."
"Help is on the way. Stay on the line with me."

Two loud booms were heard after the police and fire department arrived. Jack imagined that they breached the door to apartment 6A to rescue a choking victim. He was pretty sure that Angelo would be the only one choking after the cops found a shitload of Fentanyl laced Heroin and paraphernalia in plain view and admissible due to the *Emergency Exception*. Moreover, they would have been sure to find Adam's lifeless corpse with the memento from Angelo's apartment. He thought he would have been satisfied with the outcome, considering that Angelo appeared to be a low-level dealer that could barely scrape together a few bundles of dope. Jack immediately began to second-guess his decision as he tried to imagine the countless lives destroyed by Angelo's drug dealing. From that moment forth, Jack knew that death was the only retribution to be dealt.

4

The Reveal

Saturday brunch often brought large crowds to Bedford Avenue. Jack sat outside finishing off his eggs sipping his coffee when his phone suddenly rang.

"Hi, Daddy."

"Hi, honey," Jack excitedly said as he sat up with perfect posture.

"What are you doing?"

"Just thinking about you."

"We just came back from the beach, I made a humongous sand castle."

"That's wonderful," Jack said while pondering

how great it would have been to see Isabel

playing on the beach.

"Did you build a moat too?"

"Hello?" Jack asked prior to a pause of silence.

"It's me, Lauren."

"How are you?"

"I need you to send some extra money."

"You're getting the child support checks right?"

"I need to buy her a new bedroom set and

Johnny isn't working right now".

"Whatever, I'll write you a check."

"Alright then, say goodbye to your father."

"Goodbye Daddy. I love you!" Isabel exclaimed.

"I love you too. Don't ever forget that."

"I won't Daddy."

Jack then hung up the phone and finished his

coffee as he watched young families bustling

past the sidewalk. Jack decided to take a walk down to the park. The weekends always brought an eclectic culmination of people. Tattooed hipsters reminiscent of 1950s pinup girls were scattered across the grass adjacent to the doggy park. Jack then took a seat on a bench. He took a strong pull of his cigarette and swigged his coffee after exhaling. He couldn't help but notice a woman in her early 30s with pale white skin and tattoos covering about fifty percent of her curved body. She was sitting upright on her towel approximately five feet away from Jack's bench and her eyes pierced through Jack like he wasn't even there.

"Do you mind?" she asked.

"No, you are good where you are."

"No, do you mind smoking? You can't smoke in this park."

"I apologize if I offended you. What's your name?"

"Nunya," she sarcastically exclaimed.

"No need to be rude."

"It's Melissa."

"Pleased to meet you."

"I wish I could say the same, just kidding."

"Say, would it be possible to take you out for a drink sometime or does alcohol offend you too?"

"Sounds interesting," she said as she shuffled through her purse

She scribbled down her name and number then handed it to Jack. He took the piece of paper in his hand as he used the other to nod and tilt his shades downward in an effort to show his twinkling hazel eyes.

After spending a few hours on the waterfront watching the haziness of the skyline, his phone rang. It was Tito.

"You heard what happened to Angelo?" Tito frantically asked.

"No, what are you talking about?"

"The cops raided his house and locked him up. His runner wound up overdosing and they pinned that shit on him."

"Damn. You got another connect with quality work? People are loving that dog food." He knew everyone on the streets loved that nickname for Heroin because it wouldn't arouse suspicion if overheard.

"I had this other guy on the block, Angelo's cousin Ed, but he hasn't been picking up his phone. It's a little hot right now so things might be a little dry."

"Don't tell me that Tito, make it happen. I'm about due to re-up."

"I'll see who's around."

"Good," Jack said authoritatively.

Truth be told, Jack knew he was a little brazen in the way he spoke to Tito but his plan had worked. Jack intimidated Tito. His no frills and no bullshit attitude made the point that he was a force not to be fucked with. He had cultivated that skill as a UC. It was quintessential that the bad guys knew you weren't some chump. It could cost you your life. You also didn't want to be too aggressive because it could yield the same result.

Jack found himself waiting in the park down the block from Tito's house. It was about five days after he had last spoke to Tito. His last interaction with Tito after their last phone call was about an hour ago via text. "I got some new shit. Meet me at the park next to the bridge's bicycle path."

You never know what is going to happen next in this drug game. It can be business as usual one minute or someone with a gun in your face attempting to rob you, murder you, or both. Jack had his hands in his jeans pocket with one hand around the grip of his snub nose .38 when Tito appeared into his line of sight.

"I don't know what the fuck is going around here, people are dropping like flies in the neighborhood," Tito said as he took a seat on the bench next to Jack.

"How many plates of food?"

"Same as usual, One-Hundred," Tito responded as he handed Jack a black shopping bag.

Jack then took his grip off the .38 and retrieved a rubber banded knot of hundreds.

"Who's dope is this?" Jack asked as he peered at the unstamped glassines of heroin within the bag.

"Some new guy on the block. Flaco his name."

"Bring me around Flaco next time, I wanna order up and am tired of paying taxes."

"What?"

"Have Flaco break you off a finder fee but if I'm gonna continue to fuck with you, I need a better deal."

Jack walked up and over toward the *Chief* before Tito could process Jack's last request. Tito wouldn't have disagreed either. He knew what was good for him.

Melissa told Jack about this little meatball restaurant that she loved in the neighborhood. He only lived a few blocks away but decided to take the *Chief* out anyway. The cars were parked bumper to bumper on the block so he brought it up onto the sidewalk in front of the restaurant. He had made it a point to get there twenty minutes early as to not keep a lady waiting. She was already there wearing a red dress with matching cherry red lipstick. He approached the bar and greeted her. She gave him a hug and left a remnant of her cherry red lips right upon his cheek.

"What are you drinking?"

"Dirty martini."

"That's that gourmet stuff, huh?"

"Very funny," she said before offering him a sip.

"Dirty martini," Jack yelled amidst the Friday night crowd.

"Coming right up," said the bartender as he theatrically flipped a bottle.

They sat at that bar until the barkeep started mopping and putting the chairs up on the bar.

"You want to go for a ride?" Jack asked.

"No, I'm not sleeping with you tonight."

"I mean on a motorcycle," Jack said while smirking. He was unable to discern the last time he smiled so hard. It was rejuvenating for him to feel desired again. It took one swift kick to get the *Chief* running again. Melissa adjusted Jack's helmet upon her head as she ran her pointy nails enamored with red decor across Jack's midsection and grabbed on tight. Once over the Williamsburg Bridge they rode through the lower east side and all through lower Manhattan. Before they knew it, the sun began to reveal its radiance through the suspension cables of the Brooklyn Bridge. Melissa clutched onto Jack a little tighter as he opened up the throttle down the roadway. Ease overcame Jack as those moments of serendipity relinquished the agony. Even if it was just for a few moments.

"I had a good time last night."

"You mean this morning?" Jack teased as an older woman jogged past with her Boston terrier.

"Whatever it was, it was magical," she said as she reached over and kissed Jack on the cheek, as he stayed mounted on the *Chief*. A halo of cherry red lipstick transposed unto his cheek. "I'll be in touch."

The phone rang around mid-afternoon and woke Jack. He sat up in his bed as he stretched his free arm.

"Flaco said it's fine to bring you but he only deals with five sleeves or better," said Tito.

"What prices are we working with?"

"Four-Hundi a sleeve," street terminology for Four-Hundred Dollars for one-hundred glassines.

"Where we linking up?"

"Meet me at the corner of South Dos and Havemeyer at ten o'clock."

"See you then."

"He never saw it coming," Jack said to himself as he sat on the park's bench wiping the beads of sweat from his face. His handkerchief was soaked with sweat and remnants of the other guy's blood. Jack had gotten the drop on the last dealer, Rob the Chef, as he was closing up his noodle restaurant for the night. Jack figured that he could take out another target prior to his scheduled rendezvous with Tito.

Tito approached wearing a black hooded sweatshirt accompanied with all black garb. "Flaco's is down the block. He is looking forward to meeting you," Tito said as they walked down South Fifth Street. Jack heard the crank of a bicycle winding a few yard behind them as they walked up to a four-story walk-up. The man riding the freestyle bike three sizes too small for him made a U-turn once Jack turned his head. He and Jack had locked eyes and the feeling of uneasiness began to set in. "Something is off," Jack thought as he followed Tito up the front stairs of the apartment building. "Tito's eyes are usually popping out of his head whenever we link up to make a buy. He will scope everyone and everything out," Jack thought to himself as he briskly walked to keep up with Tito. Once inside the vestibule, Jack quickly scanned for a camera and saw that the coast was clear. He pulled his nine-millimeter semi-automatic pistol that was crowned with a silencer almost the same size as the weapon's slide and pushed it into Tito's kidney.

"What the fuck are you doing?"

"You are trying to set me up?"

"I wouldn't do you dirty, we are making money. Things are good between us."

"Keep lying and I will shoot you in the face. Your own mother won't be able to recognize you as your family kneels beside your casket."

"Listen Jack, it's nothing personal. Please don't kill me. I owe Flaco some money and he told me my debt would be clear if I help set you up," Tito cried.

"You have one chance to live, are you ready to listen?"

"I'll do anything you say."

"Get me inside and do not raise him up."

"I can do that."

Jack tucked his gun back into the rear of his waistband and turned the interior vestibule doorknob as he pushed Tito leading him forward through the entrance. Tito looked over to Jack for a verification of approval once standing in front of Apartment 3C. Jack retrieved his weapon and sandwiched it between both Tito and himself, as it lay flat across his sternum in the *sul position* (a shooting stance). Jack then nodded over to Tito in an approving manner.

"I'm coming," yelled an anticipating voice.

Flaco opened the door and Tito took a step forward while Jack trailed immediately behind with his finger relaxed against the trigger. Flaco's eyes widened with fear as he read the expression from Tito's emotionless face. Jack pushed the door closed with his left hand as he used his right hand to draw the weapon past Tito's ear and fire a shot into Flaco's face. The silencer muffled all but the sound of the pistol's mechanics and the thud from Flaco's body hitting the living room floor. A heavy set man then emerged into the hallway from the kitchen to investigate the peculiar sounds but fortunately for Jack, he was only armed with a gallon of chocolate chip ice cream and a spoon. The only problem was that he made a slightly louder thud after two bullets pierced through the ice cream container and into his chest. Jack utilized Tito's body as a shield to tactically clear the apartment.

"Please don't kill me," begged Tito after being thrown on the couch. Jack then dug his hand in his pocket and removed a handful of glassine envelopes emblazoned with a variety of colored stamps. Each stamp represented a dealer from Williamsburg that recently descended south into the fiery pits of hell. "Your name is as good as gold around here. The dealers in the neighborhood had no qualms with selling to me after I told them I knew you," Jack said.

"Diablo," Tito gasped as his eyes widened in a moment of revelation.

"Who sells the *Red Dragon*? Think long and hard."

"I never heard of it before, I swear on my children."

"Who run's shit over here? Who controls the dope on the South Side?"

"It's some guy that they call the doctor. It's not just his handle on the streets, I think he's actually a doctor. I told you all I know. Please don't kill me!" Tito begged.

Jack then took a seat next to Tito and whispered, "You will meet Diablo soon enough."

He removed a loaded hypodermic needle from his pocket. There was enough fentanyl packed inside to kill a horse. He removed the needle cap with his teeth while he teased and tormented Tito with the muzzle of the silencer. A tinge of blood gushed inside the needle's chamber once the plunger was slightly retracted. Tito's mouth began to drop and his eyes fell into oceanic depths as Jack inserted the hot dose into the carotid artery.

Jack wiped off the pistol with his shirt and placed it on the sofa cushion near Tito's lifeless hand. As he walked toward the front door, he looked back to analyze and admire the crime scene. It appeared that Tito, a drug addict with an extensive drug possession and sale history shot Flaco and the heavyset fellow in a drug related robbery. Flaco succumbed to an overdose while sampling his newly acquired product. Case opened and closed.

Jack's thoughts began to spin in tandem with the wheels of his motorcycle. The chances of finding the *Red Dragon* and the dealer that sold his brother the final dose were slim but he reminded himself that he knew that all along. Dealers periodically change stamps if the law is trailing behind. Sometimes, they just stop using a particular stamp for arbitrary or whimsical reasons. At the end of the day, he was in the right place with the right people. There were eleven dealers that met their maker. Jack rationalized that the lives of those demons were worth a minutia of value when considering the lives they would have ruined. Those lives included mothers, fathers, children, brothers, and sisters. The wind ricocheted off his teeth as he smiled in elated thought of this as he pushed through the gears.

5

Breakfast Conversation

The compass of the heart brought Jack to Melissa's apartment after the rendezvous at Flaco's. The lights to her apartment turned on as he dismounted from his steel horse. "She must have heard the bike," Jack thought. He continued up the front stairs as she yanked open the front door and ran down the stairs until she met Jack midway. She grabbed the lapels of his leather jacket as she swung her bare feet around him. Melissa feverishly kissed him as if she had been waiting for him all her life.

Jack awoke the following morning alongside Melissa. He laid there and gazed upon her exposed body in admiration when he noticed her sullied foot. He initially thought that her foot got dirty from running outside barefoot but then realized that she had collapsed veins and healed injection sores between her toes.

"Why do the damned attach themselves to me?" he asked himself.

Melissa began to toss and turn as the expanse of her eyes flickered open.

"Good morning."

"Good morning," Jack reluctantly said.

"What's wrong? Did I do something wrong? Was it too soon?"

Jack consolingly rubbed his hand down her smooth leg and began to cradle her foot as he stared into her soul. It wasn't a deal breaker but he needed an explanation, Jack thought.

"It's a reminder of my past life and what I'll never go back to," Melissa adamantly swore.

"I won't ask why you had blood spattered on your shirt last night but I'll be more than happy to explain my past and my sobriety over breakfast," she continued.

"Only if you promise to make pancakes," Jack said.

"Deal."

The sun peered through the kitchen blinds with laser point precision as Melissa began cracking eggs and preparing the mix. Jack stared at her in her over sized T-shirt as she mixed the batter. At first he began to think about how cute she looked in that shirt that was three sizes too large until he started to ponder how she happened to acquire the shirt. Was it an old boyfriend's shirt or was it her dad's? Perhaps it was her brother's shirt before it was forced to withstand the test of time and fade away as we all must. Neither the lineage of the shirt nor the identity of her past flames really concerned him. It was just fact that he spent his career paying attention to the fine details. It was an attribute that made him a good detective yet conversely it made him dwell on inconsequential issues that sometimes weighed down the mind and soul.

"I don't really know motorcycles and all but I feel like I've seen your bike before," Melissa said as she cut her pancakes in fours.

"Really, where?"

"I can't really put my finger on it but I know I have seen that rusty red color with the gold headdress painted on."

"Not too many of them like that left."

Although Jack told her matter of factly, blood began to rush through his mind. "Did she know Christopher?" He knew it was a question he needed to ask but not just yet, at this moment. He was glad to have her company and he already brought up a hot button issue regarding her scars.

"These are by far the best pancakes I've had."

"You probably say that to all the girls that make you pancakes after sleeping with you on the second date."

"No, you're the only one that has made me pancakes. Most of them aren't too crafty in the kitchen," Jack quipped. Melissa burst into a fit of laughter and as the last laugh bellowed, her facial expression became emotionless.

"About my scars..." Melissa abruptly said and then paused. I got in a pretty bad car accident about three years ago. I had some muscle spasms but besides that, I was okay. The MRIs and X-Rays showed nothing wrong but I did the whole physical therapy thing." After about two weeks after I started therapy, I was still in discomfort and they recommended a pain management doctor. His name was Dr. Smith." She began to sob.

"You don't have to continue. I can tell the wound is still fresh and I don't want you to be upset after a night of incredible sex followed up by delicious pancakes," Jack said while cracking a smirk at his own lame joke.

"I've learned through my recovery that I need to be one-hundred percent honest with myself and those I care for." Melissa wiped away her tears with the oversized sleeve of her T-shirt then placed her arm on the table. Jack placed his hand over her hand and slid his fingers through hers until he was unable to discern where his tattooed hands ended and hers began.

"So I go to Dr. Smith and on the first day he prescribes me oxycodone and alprazolam. The pills made the pain go away and before I knew it, I couldn't stop. I began to not feel like myself without those damn pills. After a month, I go back to his office to get another prescription and he tells me that he can't but that he would make an exception for me and charge me five hundred dollars for a prescription. I agreed and paid for about three months when I started chasing the dragon. That's when you…"

"Smoke the pills with foil and a lighter. I'm familiar," Jack continued as Melissa looked in slight astonishment that he was privy to the nuances of smoking pills.

"So I was broke and couldn't afford buying these scrips. I knew some people would sell their pills for twenty-five bucks so I would get them like that until one day I was leaving Dr. Smith's office and this guy offered me heroin. It was a third of the price and would make me three times higher. Eventually, I began injecting it and I didn't recognize who I was anymore. I checked into rehab and have been clean for four hundred days."

"You are amazing," Jack professed as they locked eyes.

"So are you."

The lull of the wind blowing leaves across the expanse of trees was all they could hear as they laid on a patch of grass in the park during the twilight hours of the crisp autumn night. Jack and Melissa were involved in deep conversation about nothing and everything as they often did when Melissa suddenly had an epiphany as they moved onto the topic of motorcycles.

"I remember where I saw your bike!" Melissa exclaimed.

"My brother used to ride everywhere. You probably saw it around town."

"I saw it at Dr. Smiths office," Melissa responded. Jack's heart sank as she preceded to describe Christopher.

"The rider was handsome and had blonde hair that fell down to his shoulders. He usually wore a shirt and tie with a café-racer leather jacket," Melissa said.

"That was my kid brother, Christopher," Jack said in a somber voice as he closed his eyes.

There was a break in the conversation and neither Jack nor Melissa said a word for a long while.

Jack's voice crackled as he mustered enough strength to cut through the awkward silence. "Your sobriety means the world to me," Jack said as he contently gazed in Melissa's eyes while softly gripping her chin. "I need your help but it may be too much to ask."

"I would do anything for you," Melissa contended as the expanse of her pupils begged to be enlisted in any task at hand. Although, Jack had discussed his past with Melissa, he omitted that some people would call him a serial killer. Jack was in love but he knew that a secret was no longer a secret once you told someone. Jack gave her the abridged version that included that he was looking for answers with those responsible for Christopher's death. Melissa understood that it was his grieving process and she sympathized for she was also grieving…. Grieving from the inequities of her past life although she was rebuilding a new life…a life with Jack.

Jack had devised a plan for her to go back to Dr. Smith's office in an attempt regain a rapport with him as they related to his illicit side hustle of selling prescriptions. She would go there another two or three times and establish herself as regular customer. She would then introduce Jack as a moneyman that was interested in buying prescriptions as well. The plan as Jack described, would allow him to gain Dr. Smith's confidence and perhaps, just perhaps, he would be able to voluntarily extract culpable statements from him.

"And then what…bring it to the cops?" Melissa asked.

"Yeah. I'll wear a recorder and turn it over to the cops." Jack couldn't help but feel guilty as he lied to Melissa but he knew he could not reveal his secret agenda. "Are you with me?" he asked.

"If you aren't living on the edge, you're taking up too much space," joked Melissa, although she really wasn't. She and Jack both shared insatiable hunger for the same drug of choice… Adrenaline laced with vengeance.

6

Back In The Day

The November leaves blanketed the streets in a spectrum of color on the Thanksgiving Eve of 1997. Christopher controlled the rolling thunder under his feet like the almighty Zeus himself when he was on his skateboard. It was the one thing that brought Jack and Christopher together although Jack was a senior and his kid brother just started high school.

"Great 50-50 grind Christopher," Jack cheered. "The landing could have been a little better." "Don't be so hard on yourself. I busted my ass the last time I tried that."

"I'm gonna walk over to the bathrooms and bust a leak," Jack advised.

"Why don't you just piss in the corner?"

"I get stage fright," Jack chuckled. "Besides, there are mad people out here."

Christopher gave his brother a thumbs up prior to peddling his board to perfect his technique on the steep waxed curb. Christopher ollied up the curb and slammed those trucks across the expanse of old wax like it was his job. His rear foot was situated a little too far back on the tail and he fell backwards as his board went flying into a few kids that were blowing down a blunt on a bench a few yards away. They were pumping *Biggie Smalls* out of a boom box that was knocked over when the board came crashing into it. Two of the kids approached Christopher as the third stayed behind while he puffed the rest of the blunt. Christopher recognized one of the kids from Jack's chemistry class. Just as Christopher was orienting himself with this newly discerned fact, he got sucker punched right in the jaw. He fell down on the pavers as the accomplice kicked him in the stomach while down. It was the first fight he had ever been in and he was overcome with adrenaline as he lay there on the floor in the fetal position waiting for the next blow from the gum soled construction boot. There was a second where Christopher thought that the loud thud was from the boot stomping him into the pavers once more. It wasn't for it was the sound of Jack's board whipping across the face of Jack's fifth period classmate. The deck of the skateboard cracked from the collision and Jack dropped the board. The other kid came charging towards Jack but was abruptly met with Jack's sneaky right hook. Christopher felt as if he was pulled from the depths of murky water as he clutched onto Jack's hoody while being carried onto his feet. The brothers didn't know if it was the *Chocolate Thai* chronic or the fear of seeing both of his friends get their asses kicked that paralyzed the kid on the bench but he just looked down as his defeated brethren rolled in pain against the pavers adorned with autumn's leaves.

"Let's grab a burger and some fries at the diner," Jack insisted to Christopher as he picked up the salvageable parts of his skateboard from the ground. Christopher nodded up and down in agreement as he pressed his hand against his bloody nose.

Christopher poured ten-seconds worth of sugar in to his coffee from the sugar canister as Jack puffed his cigarette while selecting American Pie on the mini jukebox along side the booth.

"I thought they were going to kill me."

"I will always have your back. You are my kid brother and I will never let anything bad happen to you," Jack implored.

"This has got me thinking. If anything were to ever happen to either one of us, how would we know if the other made it?"

"Made it where?" Jack asked with a bewildered impression as he put out his cigarette in the golden foil ashtray.

"You know," Christopher paused. "To heaven."

Jack laughed as he ruffled his brother's hair.

"I don't know. I'll give you some kind of eerie cryptic sign at a diner, a dump just like this one.

Just go to the nearest diner, order a grilled cheese, and I'll do something extravagant." Jack laughed as Christopher blushed with the embarrassment of asking a silly question.

"You guys ready for the check?" asked Martine, the waiter that usually covered the booths in the back.

"More coffee please," Jack insisted as he grabbed his cup that was quarter way filled with sugar that had reached the consistency of applesauce after five refills.

"What the fuck, all you guys do is sit here for hours and just drink free refills and smoke cigarettes. Don't you have a video game to play at home?" Martine quipped. Christopher extended his empty coffee cup implying he wanted another refill as well.

"I got you guys a fresh pot," Martine said as he poured the coffee in to Jack's cup. Christopher removed his cup from beneath the table as he shoveled out the buildup of sugar onto the floor. Martine failed to take notice and poured Christopher's coffee once he presented the cup.

"You know mom is gonna flip when she sees that black eye."

"Yeah, I know," Christopher said as he tried to examine his bruised eye in the reflection of the jukebox glass.

"We might as well get going but not before I show you a neat trick."

"What's that?" Christopher asked.

"We are just gonna play a little prank on Martine. It's what he gets for being such an asshole," Jack said as he began to unscrew the top of the sugar canister. He then placed a napkin over the top of the canister to contain the sugar while he flipped the canister and placed it in the center of the table.

"Now we just lay the metal piece on."

They walked out front and posted up in the bus shelter where they had a line of sight of the booth in which they had previously been sitting. They peered through the paned glass and saw Martine meticulously wipe down the table with a cloth. He then placed his hand on the sugar canister in an effort to move it to the side of the table adjacent to the rest of the condiments at which time the sugar covered the table. They could read the profanities pouring from Martine's mouth as he threw his rag in a fit of rage. They ran off and laughed the whole way back home.

7

<u>Doctor Visit</u>

Jack sat in the pickup drinking his piping hot coffee, his binoculars honed in on Dr. Smith's office. It was seven in the morning yet there was pretty significant foot traffic in front of the office. There was also a larger fellow standing in the front of the location that must have been security, based on his disciplined yet brooding facial expression. All the zombies walking in and out of the office appeared to be victims of the opioid apocalypse. Melissa's tiny red car prudently pulled in to a parking spot adjacent to the office at approximately 7:30 in the morning just as Melissa and Jack had planned. The receptionist in the office told Melissa that Dr.

Smith had no available appointments for the next two months but Melissa was persistent that the receptionist ask Dr. Smith if he could squeeze her in. According to the receptionist, Dr. Smith said Melissa could come in whenever she would like.

Melissa waited in the crowded waiting room for no longer than two minutes when the receptionist called her name.

"Dr. Smith is ready for you," said the bleach blonde secretary dressed in medical scrubs. Melissa thanked the receptionist as she walked her to a room situated at the end of the hallway. "The doctor will be right in," the receptionist said while opening the door to the room. Melissa sat in a chair alongside a medical table.

"How are you dear?" Dr. Smith asked as he closed the door shut behind him.

"Everything is good."

"It's been a few years, where have you been?"

"I just moved back to Brooklyn a few weeks ago. I had been staying with my folks upstate. My dad wasn't doing too well."

"Well, you are always welcome here. What do you need?"

"Percs and Oxys," Melissa said as she handed Dr. Smith a grand in crisply minted hundreds.

"It's twelve-hundred for two prescriptions but I'll take what you got. Just get me next time," advised the doctor. He penned the prescriptions on his pad and handed them to her. "I'll see you soon, Doll," Dr. Smith said as he winked in a cheesy yet flirtatious way.

Melissa hopped in the passenger side of Jack's truck at the prearranged location. It was a clandestine little spot in the back of a pharmacy.

She had to fill the prescription as to not arise suspicion for he could easily find out if he did a little digging. After all, she appeared out of nowhere a few years later to visit her dirty doctor in the hope of acquiring unwarranted prescriptions. Once inside the truck, she kissed Jack on the lips and immediately started crying.

"What's wrong? Are you okay?"

"It's just brought back a lot of memories. Going through the motions again just reminded me of the darkest of times."

"I understand and we can just forget the whole thing. It was a foolish idea to get you involved," Jack wholeheartedly said while taken aback by Melissa's pain and frailty. "You don't have to go through with this, it was selfish of me to get you involved."

"I got this. I want this piece of shit to pay for what he did to me."

"Are you sure?"

"I've never been so sure of anything," Melissa contended as she wiped away her tears. "We might have a problem introducing you though. I could barely get an appointment and I was left with the impression that he wasn't taking on new customers."

"Call the office next week to make an appointment. When you get there, tell him that your boyfriend sold those pills in three days and ask if it's okay to bring me around. The one thing that makes the bad guys rule against their better judgment is greed and the fact that they know scared money don't make money."

'I can do that."

"That reminds me. There is something I need to talk to you about. I need to start moving

Christopher's things from the apartment, the lease is up at the end of the month."

"Where are you gonna go?"

"I'm gonna head down to Florida to be closer to Isabel after I take care of this thing with the doc. There is one more thing." Jack paused. "I want you to come with me."

"I would love to," Melissa said with a sigh of relief.

They spent the next few days moving Christopher's belongings into a storage container in the Rockaways. Melissa's mind was set and she was prepared to start a new life down in Florida with Jack.

Jack and Melissa had arrived at Jack's parents house for Sunday dinner. Maria made steak and eggs for dinner with a side of Spanish potatoes.

"The food was exceptional, Maria. Thank you for having me."

"It's a pleasure to have you here. Jack has spoken very highly of you. I just wish he had brought you around sooner," Maria responded.

"I hear you plan on heading down to Florida with Jack," Manuel added as he removed a piece of steak from his teeth with a toothpick. Melissa glanced over at Jack and smiled.

"Yeah, I'm really excited to get away with Jack and meet Isabel. He misses her so much and I can't wait to meet her. She's an adorable little girl that needs her daddy around."

"I haven't seen my own granddaughter in months because she is down there with her crackhead mother and some stranger. Jack, go down there and raise your child," Manny said.

"You know, they have good blue marlin fishing down there, Dad."

"Yeah, I'm retiring from the factory in two years and then I'm selling this house and getting the fuck out of here. It's time to relax after busting my ass all these years. In fact, I'm going to buy a motorcycle too when we get down there."

"You are not getting a motorcycle," Maria exclaimed as she scolded Manny while waving her finger in his face. Everyone began to laugh and the culmination of laughter and conversation resonated throughout the evening.

8

Smoke'em If you Got'em

Melissa sat patiently in the waiting room chair of Doctor Smith's office. The office was so quiet that she could hear the hum of the fluorescent light fixtures. Although there were a handful of people in the office, the patients sat in stillness as they waited patiently for the doctor to satiate their opiate induced euphoria. The destruction of opiate abuse was transparently obvious on the faces of those waiting. Melissa's imagination ran off as she imagined how they appeared to be recipients of a lobotomy. She was sure glad she hadn't gotten to that point.

"Melissa," called the receptionist. She got up from her seat and walked through in to the room.

"How are you darling?" asked Dr. Smith.

"I'm great, I need to fill those prescriptions."

"That was quick."

"My boyfriend has a lot of friends. In fact, he wanted me to ask if he could come see you," Melissa nervously asked.

"I'm no longer taking any more patients."

"Dr. Smith…"

"I told you. I'm not taking any more patients. In fact, you are lucky that I'm taking care of you. So let's get to it. You want the same order as last week?" Doctor Smith asked as he looked through a spiral bound notepad.

"That'll be fine Doctor."

"Fourteen-Hundred. You have a previous balance of two-hundred," Dr. Smith said as he furiously wrote on his prescription pad. Melissa was taken aback not only by how much of an asshole he was, but also how straight to the point he was when it came to money.

"Hope to see you soon, Darling," he said after Melissa handed him a small stack of hundreds.

"Be well, Doctor Smith," Melissa said with artificial composure. Her rage was masked in the name of revenge.

She picked up her phone and called Jack once she secured the prescriptions in the glove box.

"Hello."

"Can you believe this asshole?"

"What happened?"

"He asked how I sold the pills so quick and I told him that my boyfriend has a lot of connections. I proceeded to tell him that you wanted to meet him."

"What did he say?"

"He became so angry and adamant that he wasn't taking on any new customers. Then he told me that I'm basically lucky that he is hitting me off."

"Don't worry about it baby, you tried your best."

"You wanna meet me at the pharmacy again?"

"No, I just gotta finish getting a few things over to storage."

"I'll give you a call tonight when I'm done."

"I'm sorry I couldn't get the job done, Jack. Don't be upset with me," pleaded Melissa.

"You tried your best. We can't force it. Let's just put it past us and tighten up what we have to tighten up here. We are gonna hit the road and put all this shit behind us."

They said their goodbyes and Jack's mind began to drift. He had spent the past few days surveilling Dr. Smith and studying his routines, his every movement. Dr. Smith would be his last hoorah before he hit the road. Jack popped a cigarette in to his mouth and flicked open his lighter. He spun the spark wheel in tandem with his mind as the flame engrossed the tip of the cigarette

"Goodnight Dr. Smith."

"Goodnight Suzy," he waved as he walked out of the office clutching the handle of his briefcase with one hand and suit jacket in the other.

Once inside the parking garage, he turned around abruptly as he heard the beat of footsteps trailing behind. To his relief, it was just an elderly man weighted down with shopping bags walking to his car. The doctor was extra cautious and paranoid these days and rightfully so. His sordid medical practice was quite reputable amongst junkies and stickup boys alike. He hopped in his *Jag* and started the trek home to suburbia in Suffolk Long Island with the top down.

The colored leaves drifted across the tree-lined streets as Dr. Smith pulled in to an old service station that was deserving of the name. The gas station bell chimed as it did every night when he pulled in to the station for his nightly ritual of topping off his gas tank and getting a pound cake.

"Fill it up premium," Dr. Smith directed toward the gas station attendant once the wheels came to a halt. He was fumbling through his jacket pocket that rested on the seat of the fine Corinthian leather in an attempt to retrieve his wallet.

"Right away, sir."

"Clean the front window too," he ordered while feeling the jacket pocket. "Where the hell did I put my wallet," he mumbled to himself.

"Sure thing, Dr. Smith."

"How do you know my…?" Dr. Smith nervously asked as he looked over toward the gas station attendant.

"Give me the fucking key or I'll blow that herpe you call a head off of your shoulders," Jack ordered as Dr. Smith stared down the muzzle of the pistol. He then handed Jack the key and pleaded with him to put the gun down. Jack then holstered his weapon and began to douse Dr. Smith's poplin shirt with gasoline.

"Make a right at the next traffic light," Jack ordered as he got in to the passenger seat. Jack retrieved his weapon and fixated it on Dr. Smith as he handed him back the key. Once around the corner, Dr. Smith parked the car and complied with Jack's order to hand him back the key.

"Who are you and what do you want? How do you know my name?" the doctor asked.

"The man holding the gun to your head is the one that is asking the fucking questions right now. I will be sure to answer your questions in due time."

"Okay, I'm sorry."

"Do you know this person?" Jack asked while showing the doctor a photo of Christopher mounted on the *Chief*. The front sight of the pistol was still fixated at Dr. Smith's head.

"He looks familiar but I can't recall from where."

"I can tell, based off your evasive answers, that we aren't getting anywhere. I'll answer your questions instead."

"I am my brother's keeper and I know all about your crooked medical practice. I also know that you are the main heroin supplier in Williamsburg."

"You may know a lot of things, but you will never get away with this."

"Watch me," Jack said as he exited the vehicle.

Silence was accompanied only with the faint sound of a spark wheel scratching across a flint. The throbbing bass of engulfing flames and agonizing screams immediately proceeded and were followed by the intonation of a furious motor cutting across the autumn wind.

9

Moving On

Jack and Melissa were able to accomplish a lot in two short weeks. She subletted her apartment to an old college friend and Christopher's apartment sat vacant waiting for its next inhabitant. They found a quaint house that sat on a farm a few miles down from Lauren in Jupiter, Florida. Jack found comfort in that the chase was over and that the angst of vengeance was purged from his system with the promise of a new tomorrow.

The bed of the pickup was filled with Melissa's belongings and Jack just had to bring a few things that he had stowed at his folks' house. He stared in the closet of his childhood room that currently contained most of his personal effects. He took a few shirts and pairs of pants off the hangars but opted to leave the leather jacket behind for it had suited its purpose. His alter ego had a tendency to reveal itself when he wore it and it was best left buried in the closet with his dark secrets. The *Chief* found its slumber in the depths of his parent's garage. Although he was done with seeking vengeance, he didn't regret any of it for he knew that he had to become a dragon in order to chase a dragon. Jack hugged his parents goodbye and picked up his acoustic guitar along with a duffle bag containing some clothes and family photos. He didn't want to bring too much of the past because he was looking forward to the future with his girl and his daughter by his side.

Jack decided to call Isabel after a few hours on the road. Lauren picked up the phone and something about her was different. It was the first time in a long time that she was actually pleasant to talk to. Lauren expressed that she was glad that Jack had found someone to settle down with. After a little small talk, she put Isabel on the phone.

"Hi, Daddy."

"Hey honey," I am on my way down to Florida.

"Are you going to Disney world?" Isabel asked with a hint of jealousy.

"No, I am going down there to be with you. In fact, I will live right down the road from you."

"I am so happy. I missed you so much."

"I missed you too, my love."

"Ok, my show is on now, I'll talk to you later."

"I'll talk to you later. I love you," Jack responded but the phone had hung up before he could finish.

The pickup continued on down the interstate nestled in between an eternity of trees that blocked out the rest of the world. Time would have stood still if it wasn't for the pavement markings that sped past the pickup amidst the autumn twilight. Jack knew that exact moment would be forever engrained in his psyche. There wasn't a word spoken at that moment in time for they were both enthralled with the serendipitous gift.

Darkness had settled in and Melissa was sound asleep. Jack started to fatigue after all those hours on the road and the signs that signified a rest stop was approaching caused him to indulge in the temptation to stop and rest. The pickup pulled into the rest stop and the country music playing from the radio faded out. He found comfort in the sound of the crickets and the rhythm of breath that sounded through Melissa's cherry red lips. He had just fallen into the depths of his sleep when he was awakened by a loud bang in the bed of the pickup. He looked over at Melissa but she was still sound asleep. The driver side mirror captured a foot in its view. Jack recovered his .38 from the gap in between the center console and his seat and opened the door. As soon as Jack approached the rear of pickup bed, he saw a man rummaging through his belongings. His partner had Jack's guitar case in his hand. The man that was attempting to steal his guitar dropped the case on the ground and pulled out a bowie knife. The other man jumped down from the bed of the pickup and they both approached Jack.

"Drop it, motherfucker," Jack ordered while pointing his .38 revolver at the head of the knife wielding thief. The stillness of night caused the dropped knife sound to echo.

"Now put my belongings back where you found them," Jack demanded with the .38 now pressed into the thief's eye socket. His partner began to gently place the guitar case and luggage back into the bed of the pickup.

"The old me would have killed your ass but I suppose I've turned over a new leaf.

Say….that's a nice cowboy hat you got there. You a cowboy?" Jack asked while staring into the depths of the man's eyes.

"No, I'm no cowboy," the thief mumbled.

"Hand over the hat. It's the taxes you pay for disrupting my sleep," Jack explained. The man removed his hat and slowly handed it over to Jack.

"Sorry about all this mister."

"Get the fuck outta here," Jack ordered with his heavy New York accent. The men then sprinted through the parking lot. He continued back into the driver seat and noticed Melissa was still deep in the tranquility of her sleep. He put on his newly acquired hat and lowered it over his face until he fell back into the depths of his dreams.

By the time Melissa awoke, Jack was already back on the road.

"Good morning," she said while partially yawning and stretching out her arms.

"Good morning to you too, little lady."

"Where did you get the cowboy hat from?"

"A nice older fellow gave it to me at the rest stop." Melissa incredulously glanced over at Jack until the diversion of the Floridian welcome signs captured her attention. It was more than just a sign that indicated they would finally be able to get out of that rust bucket of a truck that surprisingly didn't break down. For Melissa, it was a second chance at life in which love was her new drug of choice.

Upon arriving in Jupiter, the onshore winds blew off the Atlantic and careened past the beaten down pickup. Serenity overcame Jack as he passed the cattle grazing behind the white wooden barriers of the farmland. He couldn't help but feel as if he took the first breath of air after being submerged in the pestilence of his life back home for he had spent most of his adult years amidst the grittiness of addiction and violence. Although this new place was foreign to him, he had finally arrived home. The key was under the mat just as the realtor had said. They had rented a fully furnished ranch that would be the place where he would help raise his daughter with Melissa by his side.

Jack could have sworn that he could hear the radiance of the sun beating upon his skin as he sat on the patio chair. Melissa had taken the pickup to get linens and groceries so Isabel would be all set once she arrived at the house. Jack and Lauren had arranged that he would have Isabel for the weekend while she and her boyfriend went down to the Keys.

The sound of the tires treading over the dirt road could be heard all the way from the rear patio. The doorbell then rang and his heart skipped a beat for he knew that it must be Lauren dropping Isabel off.

"I love you so much!" Jack exalted as he wrapped Isabel in his arms.

"I'm so excited to have a sleep over at your house, Daddy."

"You can have a sleepover at your house, honey," Jack responded. Lauren rolled her eyes.

"We will be back next Monday. Make sure she doesn't stay up too late," Lauren directed as she placed two bags down. "This pink duffle bag has her clothes and the glittery bag has way too many toys that she insisted on bringing with her."

"Sounds good," Jack responded without making eye contact.

"Bye mommy."

"Goodbye sweetie," Lauren said after giving Isabel a kiss on her cheek.

"You look good, Jack."

"So do you, have a good trip," Jack said emotionlessly as he looked down at his feet.

He still wasn't over the way their marriage ended. It wasn't because it ended; it was just how it ended. Jack and Isabel waved as they drove away. He figured it was the diplomatic thing to do although he wasn't in the best place with Lauren and he utterly detested her boyfriend, Johnny. They then walked back in the house, hand in hand.

Jack looked down at Isabel and asked, "So, what do you want to do today?"

"Daddy, as long as I'm with you....I'm happy," Isabel responded as a tear began to run down the side of Jack's face.

"Where did you learn to be so sweet?" Jack asked as he wiped away his tears just in the nick of time.

"You must be Isabel!" Melissa exclaimed, as she was halfway through the door.

"Hi, who are you?"

"I'm your daddy's friend," Melissa explained as she took a knee.

"Ok, you wanna play tag?"

"I'll go grab the shopping bags," Jack said to the walls as Melissa and Isabel were engrossed in conversation.

10

Daddy's Girl

If Jack could have described the first day at the house, he would have said it was uneventful yet bliss. Melissa stocked the fridge and got the rooms ready with freshly washed linens. The trio played board games after a mac and cheese dinner and turned in early. It had been a long journey both literally and figuratively. Isabel was ready to start her day before sunrise the following morning and she wasn't shy about walking into Jack's room and waking him up. Fortunately for Melissa, she slept in the third bedroom. Jack and Melissa both agreed that the new domestic situation might be a little confusing for Isabel and they opted to sleep separately when Isabel was around, at least in the beginning.

"Do you want to go to the beach this morning, Isabel?"

"Okay, but after my show," Isabel said as she chopped away at her microwaveable pancake pouch while watching Saturday morning cartoons.

"No problem, my love," Jack responded as his starstruck eyes consumed the image of his little girl rustling her hand in the pancake pouch.

The parking lot at the beach was still empty and it seemed as if the rest of the world was still asleep. Isabel popped out of the cab with her tote bag containing beach toys in one hand and glitter backpack in the other. Jack retrieved a beach chair from the bed of the truck.

"Why don't you leave the glitter backpack in the truck, the sand might mess it up?" Jack asked insinuatingly.

"Ok, that's a good idea, Daddy," Isabel agreed as she returned the glitter backpack to the cab of the truck.

The two continued down towards the water as Isabel's flip flops got trapped in the sand every few paces. They finally stopped a few feet shy of where the sea foam met the sand. Isabel began to play with her beach toys as Jack propped himself in his beach chair. The sea foam massaged his legs in harmony with the flow of the tide. All he could see was his daughter and the slow rising sun dauntingly revealing the expanse of the sea.

People started to arrive and vendors started setting up on the beach as the morning continued on. Jack figured that Melissa should be up by now and he thought that she must have been wondering where he and Isabel had gone. Jack wiped his sandy hands on his shorts and dialed Melissa's number.

"Good morning," Jack said.

"Good morning, I just woke up."

"You want to take a cab and meet us over at the beach?"

"I still need to unpack a few things and organize the house. How about I meet you guys for lunch after you guys are done?"

"That's a great idea. I'll call you when we are getting ready to leave."

"Ok. Buh-bye."

Jack hung up the phone and told Isabel to follow him. They walked passed the vendors and saw a stand up paddleboard.

"How much to rent the paddle board?"

"Fifty-bucks for four hours," the kid behind the makeshift wooden booth responded.

Jack paid him and Isabel trailed behind the fin of the board as Jack tracked the rail along the sand. They walked into the water and Jack propped Isabel on the nose of the board. He then hopped on and balanced himself on his knees. He then began to paddle out passed the breaking waves. The swell wasn't huge but the waves had five-foot faces that would have intimidated most kids that were sitting Indian style on the nose of a paddleboard. Isabel wasn't most kids. Her eyes illuminated as they paddled over the lips of the waves that were in the initial state of collapsing. They were finally past the breakers watching the mist dissipate into the air. They had reached into a vortex where the stillness of time and sound manifested itself. They sat there for a while in silence. The bulge of a worthwhile set lurked beneath the water. Jack stood up and began to paddle the ore, as Isabel stayed seated up on the nose. The vessel was propped in the pocket of the wave as he used the ore to slow their pace once the rainbow of the sea covered them through the barrel.

Jack carried the board back to the shore with Isabel at this side. Their matching smiles were a byproduct of the sea's power and their moment together.

"I think that was the way to end a beach day, what do you think kid?"

"It was so cool."

"Yes, it was." They returned the board and rid themselves of the sand caked to the bottom of their feet with a ratty old towel. Jack called Melissa back.

"We are all set, where do you wanna meet for lunch?" Jack asked Melissa.

"Let's try that diner over on Okeechobee Road."

"Sounds simple enough. Give us fifteen minutes."

As Jack and Isabel pulled up, they saw Melissa was already waiting in the glass vestibule in front of the diner. Jack went over to the passenger side of the truck and opened the door. Isabel popped out of the cab with here glitter book bag clenched in her hands.

"How was the day at the beach?" Melissa asked while looking at Isabel.

"It was great, we were inside of a humungous wave."

"I don't even want to ask," Melissa chuckled then incredulously looked at Jack. Melissa opened the entrance door and they were greeted by the maître d'.

"Hi, how many?"

"Three," Jack replied as he held Isabel's hand. A waitress then came over then told them to follow her as she toted the heavy and ornate menus. The waitress pointed to the booth and the trio took a seat.

"What would you guys like to drink?"

"I'll have a Shirley temple," Isabel said while placing her glitter book bag on the table.

"Make that two," Melissa chimed in.

"I'm good with the water, thanks," Jack said as he looked at Melissa with a dumbfounded face.

"What? I haven't had a Shirley temple in years and I figured no better time than the present."

Jack began to crack the menu open and glance through the burger column of the menu. Isabel was unzipping her glitter book bag and fumbling through a bunch of items. She removed a box of crayons, a red inkpad, and a few rubber stamps. The tapping sound of Isabel working the stamps into the inkpad took a back seat as the sound of quarters dropping into the jukebox resonated into the cavities of Jack's ears.

"I love this song," Melissa childishly said when American Pie began to play on the jukebox. A sinister feeling of anxiety ran up Jack's neck like a bolt of electricity as his sweet Isabel lifted her stamp from the paper place mat. There it was…**the Red Dragon**.

11

A Little Less Throttle

"Welcome to Pete's Miami Cycle Center, are you looking for anything in particular?" the salesman asked as the customer entered the store.

"Me and my boy here are just gonna grab some shirts to bring back home. It's our first time down here in Miami."

"Very well, the apparel is back there in the far right of the store."

"Sure thing…. Steve," the gentleman said after leaning in to examine the salesman's name tag.

"More tourists kicking tires, Steve?" the other salesman asked as he returned back towards the counter.

"Yeah, I haven't sold a bike all week, these fucking tourists and their memorabilia. Half of them don't even own motorcycles. They just want to walk around like some asshole advertising a motorcycle company.

"Yeah, you're right. It's pretty damn hot in here, the air conditioning unit must be on the fritz again," the other salesman said as he propped open the entrance doors with doorstoppers.

A man cloaked with a black leather jacket and oil slicked jeans walked through the entrance gripping a black duffle bag. His boot steps echoed as he progressed down the sales floor while his haunted eyes fixated on the cruisers. Steve trailed behind the man as he adjusted his nametag in an effort to prep himself for a possible sale.

"Welcome to Pete's Miami Cycle Center, do you need any help with anything?" Steve asked as he approached the man.

"I'm looking for a new sled."

"Are you looking for a touring bike or something a little smaller?"

"I need something dark and fast."

"What do you think about something like this?" Steve asked with confused intonation as he pointed towards a blacked out American V-Twin.

"I'll take it," the man responded without hesitation.

I'll have the sales manager get started with the financing paperwork."

"No financing, I'm paying cash," the man said as he unzipped the duffle bag.

"With tax, it'll be eighteen-thousand even, I'll take off the freight charge," Steve said as he nervously looked down at the floor. The man then handed Steve eighteen stacks of bills bundled individually with rubber bands. A few of the stacks appeared to be specked with a dark red substance that resembled blood. Steve then handed the man in black a key fob.

"How did you hear about our dealership? Steve asked.

"Just popped in, it's the last one before I hit the Florida Keys."

"That it is. Got your trip planned out or just plan on doing some cruising and relaxation?"

"Just Chasing the Dragon."

Although bewildered by the man's response, Steve said, "Well, pleasure doing business with you, all we have left to do is fill out some paperwork for your registration. I also need a copy of your license."

"Pleasure was all mine," the man said as he threw his leg around the bike and fired up the ignition.

"You can't start the bike in the store," Steve yelled, over the howling exhaust as Jack dropped the bike in gear. The rear tire spun across the polished wood floor until it gained traction on the blacktop of the parking lot. The devil and his chariot then fled unto the southbound lanes of the interstate.

68532554R00088

Made in the USA
Lexington, KY
13 October 2017